Nicki
the Holiday Camp Fairy

by Daisy Meadows

ORCHARD

www.rainbowmagic.co.uk

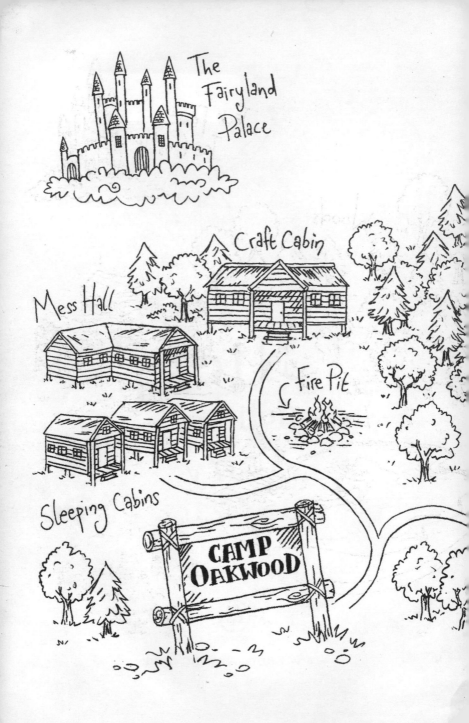

The Fairyland Palace

Craft Cabin

Mess Hall

Fire Pit

Sleeping Cabins

CAMP OAKWOOD

Nicki
the Holiday Camp
Fairy

Special thanks
to Tracey West

ORCHARD BOOKS
338 Euston Road, London NW1 3BH
Orchard Books Australia
Level 17/207 Kent Street, Sydney, NSW 2000
A Paperback Original

First published in the USA in 2011 by Scholastic Inc.
This edition published in the UK in 2013 by Orchard Books

A CIP catalogue record for this book is available
from the British Library.

ISBN 978 1 40832 512 4

1 3 5 7 9 10 8 6 4 2

Printed in Great Britain

The paper and board used in this paperback are natural recyclable
products made from wood grown in sustainable forests. The
manufacturing processes conform to the environmental regulations
of the country of origin.

Orchard Books is a division of Hachette Children's Books,
an Hachette UK company

www.hachette.co.uk

Camp Chaos!

Jack Frost's Spell

Goblins adore some things about camp,
Bugs and games and mud and damp.
But I, Jack Frost, can't stand the sun.
I sit in the dark while campers have fun.

So I'll ruin camp and drain the lake.
I'll spoil the crafts kids love to make.
As long as I have the items three,
No one will have fun but me!

Contents

Goblin Tracks

"I can't believe we're actually at holiday camp together!" Rachel Walker said happily.

"Me, neither," said her best friend, Kirsty Tate. "We get to do some of our favourite things all in one place. And we get to do them together!"

Rachel and Kirsty had met on holiday

on the beautiful Rainspell Island. Since
they lived in different towns, they didn't
get to see each other every day. So when
the girls' parents had suggested they go
to Camp Oakwood, both Rachel and
Kirsty were very excited.

Now, on their second day of camp,
the two girls sat at a table in the Craft
Cabin. They were making pictures
with wool.

"First, sketch your picture on the
paper," explained Bollie, their
camp leader. Bollie's
real name was Margaret
Bolleran, but everyone
called her Bollie.

Rachel sketched a fairy on her
paper. She looked over at Kirsty
and saw that she had sketched a

fairy, too. The girls smiled at each other.

"Now spread the glue over the places you would normally colour in," Bollie said. "Then you can curl up pieces of wool and place them on the glue, like this."

She held up a picture of a tree with green wool for leaves and brown wool on the trunk… but then the wool slid off and plopped on one of Bollie's boots.

"That's funny," she said, feeling the paper. "This glue isn't sticky at all."

"My glue isn't sticking, either," complained a red-haired girl.

Bollie frowned. "Maybe it's too hot," she said, pushing her blonde fringe out of her eyes. "I know! Let's have some fun with the paint spinner, instead."

Bollie walked to a big machine on a table at the side of the room. Rachel, Kirsty, and the other girls gathered around to watch.

"It's easy," Bollie said, her green eyes shining. "You put paper on the bottom. Then you turn on the spinner and squeeze in drops of paint."

She held a plastic bottle of orange paint over the spinner and squeezed it. With a POP! the lid flew off! Instead of just a few drops, the whole bottle of paint gushed into the spinner.

"Everybody duck!" Bollie yelled.

15

Rachel and Kirsty ducked down as
quickly as they could. Orange paint
splattered everywhere! Bollie turned
off the machine, but not before every
camper was covered in orange splodges.

"Oh, no!" some of the
girls wailed.

Rachel giggled. "It's
like we're covered in
sprinkles," she said.

But Bollie did not look
happy. "Everybody head
to the sinks to clean up!"
she told them. "Craft time is
cancelled. We're going on a hike!"

The campers quickly washed off the
paint and changed into clean green-and-
white Camp Oakwood vest tops. They
lined up at the edge of the woods.

"Follow me, and stick to the path,"
Bollie said.

Rachel and
Kirsty hung
back at the end
of the line.

"Rachel, why
do you think
that happened in
the Craft Cabin?" Kirsty
asked in a whisper.

Rachel gave her a meaningful look.
"It feels like Jack Frost to me."

Rachel and Kirsty were whispering
because they shared a big secret. They
were friends with the fairies! They
knew that wicked Jack Frost was always
playing tricks on fairies and humans
with the help of his goblins.

"But what would Jack Frost be doing at holiday camp?" Kirsty wondered. "He likes to be in the cold, doesn't he?"

Just then, Bollie stopped on the path. "Look! Here are some tracks we can examine," she said.

The campers made a circle around Bollie as she bent down to give the tracks a closer look.

"That's strange," she said. "I thought maybe they'd be deer prints or badger tracks. But these look like big, bare feet. Who would walk around the woods in bare feet?"

Rachel and Kirsty knew exactly who would do that.

Goblins!

The Secret Switch

It was hard for Rachel and Kirsty to talk about the goblins, since they had to stay with Bollie and the other campers. They had to wait until dark, when everyone gathered around a campfire for the night-time story. They sat alone at a nearby picnic table.

"Did you see those tracks?" Kirsty asked. "I'm sure that Jack Frost and his goblins are around here!"

"If they were causing trouble, wouldn't the fairies ask us to help?" Rachel wondered.

Kirsty nodded. "Maybe they don't know that Jack Frost is here."

Rachel frowned. "I wish we had some way to contact them."

"Hmmm," Kirsty said. Then her eyes lit up. "We do have fairy dust!"

The fairy dust was a present from King Oberon and Queen Titania, the fairy king and queen. Each girl carried some in a special locket. They could use the fairy dust to visit Fairyland.

"But we can't visit Fairyland now," Rachel pointed out. "Bollie would be looking for us."

Kirsty was thoughtful. "Maybe we can sprinkle it on something," she suggested. "Like a mirror or a bubble. Something that would let us see into Fairyland."

Rachel pointed to a puddle near the picnic table. "What about that?"

"Perfect!" Kirsty said.

The girls made sure no one was close by. Pale light from the moon shone on the puddle as Kirsty sprinkled some of her fairy dust.

A shimmery light beamed through the murky water, and then the faces of King Oberon and Queen Titania appeared.

"Hello, Rachel and Kirsty," said the queen. "What a pleasant surprise!"

"I'm afraid we have news that isn't so pleasant, Your Majesty,"

Kirsty said. "We think Jack Frost and his goblins are here at Camp Oakwood." The king and queen looked shocked. "We'll send Nicki the Holiday Camp Fairy to help you right away," the king said.

"Thank you so much," Rachel replied. Then the puddle went dark.

A moment later, a small group of fireflies began to circle the girls. Their yellow lights blinked on and off. Then one of the lights got bigger and brighter.

25

The light burst into glittering sparks, like a mini fireworks display.

Nicki the Holiday Camp fairy appeared in front of them! She had light-brown hair, and wore layered orange and pink tops with cropped blue jeans.

"Hey, campers!" she said cheerfully. "I hear you've had a goblin sighting."

"We saw goblin tracks!" Kirsty told her.

"And everything was messed up in the Craft Cabin today," Rachel added.

Nicki frowned. "That shouldn't have happened. I have three magical objects in here that help make camp extra-fun

for everybody." She slid her backpack off and patted it.

"Ooh, can we see them?" Rachel asked.

"Of course," said Nicki. She flew to the picnic table, opened up her backpack, and tipped the contents onto the table. Three big, grey rocks fell out.

"Oh, no!" Nicki cried. "Jack Frost's goblins must have stolen them!"

"Did you leave your backpack alone somewhere?" Kirsty wondered.

"No," Nicki said, shaking her head. "But the other day I was in the woods near Jack Frost's Ice Castle when I saw some fairies camping out. They needed help, so I showed them how to build a fire. I put my backpack down for a few minutes."

"Those fairies must have been goblins in disguise," Kirsty guessed.

Nicki nodded. "They must have secretly switched the magic items for rocks when I wasn't looking!"

"What do the magic items do?" Rachel asked.

"Each one helps give holiday camp some extra sparkle," Nicki explained. "My holiday camp bracelet helps make camp activities fun and exciting.

 My water bottle helps keep campers cool in the heat. And my last item is a compass that keeps campers from getting lost."

"That must be why the paint splattered everywhere and the glue didn't stick," Kirsty realised.

"Exactly. Because the friendship bracelet is missing," Rachel said, finishing the thought.

Nicki nervously flapped her wings. "We've got to find those goblins, fast!"

Just then, a voice cried out, "Rachel!
Kirsty! Where are you?"

Nicki waved her wand. "I should go!"

The fairy disappeared as a little girl
with short brown hair ran up. Ellie
Campbell was a few years younger than
Rachel and Kirsty, but she had latched
onto them right away.

"It's time for lights-out!" Ellie told

them. "But I'm not going to go to sleep right away, are you? I'm going to read my fairy book under the covers with my torch."

"That sounds like fun," Rachel said. "Kirsty and I like fairies, too."

Ellie beamed. "Aren't they great? I wish I could meet a real one."

Rachel and Kirsty smiled at each other. They knew how lucky they were to be friends with the fairies.

"I hope Nicki comes back soon," Rachel whispered as they walked back to their cabin.

"Me, too," Kirsty said. "If we don't get those magic items back, holiday camp will be ruined!"

Camp Frost

The girls at Camp Oakwood slept in rustic wood cabins. Each one was filled with bunk beds. Rachel and Kirsty shared a cabin with five other girls their age. Their group was called the Fun Foxes.

The next day, after breakfast, the

camp leaders gathered the Fun Foxes,
the Happy Hedgehogs and the Merry
Mice by the sparkling lake. They were
going to take a canoe trip. A row of
canoes was tied to posts on the dock.

"Hmm. The lake looks a little low
today," Bollie was saying to another
leader.

"It's deep enough for canoeing," said
a different leader, a woman with dark
brown plaits.

Bollie blew her whistle.
"Okay, Fun Foxes!
We're taking these two
canoes. Please put on
your life jackets now."

"I've never been in a canoe
before," said Kirsty, as she slipped on her
orange life jacket.

"It's like being in a yacht, only we get to row," Rachel told her. "It's fun!"

Bollie and the other leaders stepped into their canoes first.

"Okay," Bollie said. "Please get into the canoe one at a time. No jumping, or you'll rock the boat!"

Rachel stepped in first. As she stepped forwards, her foot sloshed in a puddle of water.

"Bollie, is it supposed to be wet in here?" Rachel asked.

"Our canoe is leaking, too!" called another leader.

"So is ours!" called someone else.

Bollie shook her head. "It seems like nothing is going right today." She blew her whistle. "Okay, campers, you've got one hour of free time!"

Rachel climbed out of the canoe. "My trainers are squishy," she told Kirsty.

"It's because of Nicki's missing holiday camp bracelet," Kirsty said in a low voice.

"Nicki said its magic helps make camp activities fun and exciting. So far, almost every activity has been ruined!"

"Then I know how we should spend our free time," Rachel said. "We need to find Jack Frost."

Kirsty nodded. Then she noticed a bright glint at the edge of the woods. She nudged Rachel. "I think it's fairy magic. Look!" she said.

The girls ran towards the trees. As they got closer, they saw Nicki sitting on an oak leaf, waving her wand.

"Thank goodness you spotted me!" Nicki said.

"We have an hour of free time," Kirsty told her. "We can help you look for Jack Frost."

"But I've already found him," Nicki said, hopping off of the leaf. She grinned. "Jack Frost and his goblins are on the other side of the woods! He's set up his own camp."

"Why would he do that?" Rachel asked.

"Who knows?" said Kirsty. "But that's probably where he's keeping the magic objects!"

"Exactly," said Nicki.

"We need to get there fast," Kirsty pointed out. "We don't have much time."

Nicki waved her wand. "Then we'll fly!"

Shimmering clouds of fairy dust

sprinkled over the girls. They grew
smaller and smaller until they were
Nicki's size. Wings sprouted from their
shoulders.

"Let's go!" Nicki cried.

They flew quickly through the trees
until they came to the edge of the
woods. Then they stopped and hovered
with Nicki behind a pine tree.

"See?" Nicki said, pointing up ahead.

It looked like Jack Frost had taken over an abandoned camp. The big wooden sign used to say CAMP PINE TREE, but the words "Pine Tree" had been covered in green spray paint. Now the sign read CAMP FROST.

Goblins in Camp Frost T-shirts walked among the rundown cabins. Only one of the cabins looked shiny and new, glimmering with magic. Bright green paint covered the walls, and a huge air conditioner hummed in the front window.

"That must be Jack Frost's cabin," Kirsty guessed. "He likes it best when it's cold."

Then the girls heard a loud noise coming from one of the other cabins. It sounded like goblins yelling at each other.

"Follow me," Nicki said.

The girls flew quickly through the camp. Then they stopped on the dusty windowsill of the noisy cabin and peered inside.

"It's the goblin's craft cabin," Rachel whispered.

Paint, glue, glitter, lolly sticks, pom-

poms and lots of other craft supplies were stored on shelves around the room. A group of green goblins with long noses sat at a table, painting pictures. As usual, the goblins were arguing.

"That's my paintbrush!"

"No, I had it first!"

At another round table, some goblins were making wool pictures — or trying to. They were squirting glue on each other and wrapping each other in wool!

"Hey, their glue and paint seem to be working fine," Kirsty noticed.

"The friendship bracelet must be nearby," Nicki said. She sounded excited. She moved closer to the window.

Rachel spotted something glimmering on a shelf inside a plastic bin of friendship bracelets, coloured string, and beads. She pointed it out to Nicki.

"That's it!" the little fairy cried.

"We have to fly past the goblins to get it," Kirsty said, sighing. "They'll see us."

Rachel thought hard. "I have another idea," she said. "The goblins are always putting on disguises to fool us. Maybe we can disguise ourselves to fool them."

"Disguise ourselves as what?" Kirsty asked.

Rachel grinned. "Goblins, of course!"

Nicki's Crafty Magic

Nicki clapped her hands together. "That's perfect!"

"But where will we get goblin costumes?" Kirsty wondered.

"Crafts are my speciality," Nicki explained. "And since we're close to the special bracelet, my crafty magic should be working well."

Nicki waved her wand, and green craft paper, green wool, and tubes of green paint appeared in front of her.

Then she waved her wand again. Gold stars and leaves shot out as she sang a little song:

"Paper, wool, and paint combine!
Make two costumes that are fine.
Rachel and Kirsty will be disguised.
They'll look like goblins in everyone's eyes!"

The girls watched in amazement as the different pieces came together to make two goblin costumes: green shirts, green

tracksuit bottoms and long, green noses.
Nicki waved her wand again, and the
costumes magically appeared on the
girls, who were back to their normal size
again!

Rachel and Kirsty stared at each other
for a moment.

"We look just like goblins!" Rachel
said with a giggle.

Nicki smiled and crouched down on
the windowsill. "I'll keep watch. Good
luck, girls!"

Rachel and Kirsty were a little bit
nervous. Fairies were nice, but goblins
were another story.

The girls walked into the goblins' craft
cabin. The goblins were still yelling and
arguing as they tried to glue some lolly
sticks together.

"Jack Frost wants thirteen of these
frames," barked one of the goblins. "So
hurry up and make them!"

"But we don't know how," a goblin
whined. "It's too hard."

Just then, the big
goblin noticed Rachel
and Kirsty. "Hey,
you two!" he yelled.
The girls froze.
Could he see through
their disguises?

"What are you doing standing there? Make some picture frames!" he ordered.

"We'd better do what he wants," Rachel whispered.

The girls got to work, lining up the lolly sticks and gluing them together.

The goblin next to Rachel nudged her with his bony elbow. "Hey, you know how to do it!"

"It's easy," Rachel said, in a deep goblin voice. "I'll show you."

The girls showed the goblins how to make the frames. Soon, they weren't arguing any more. They were happily sticking away.

"This camping stuff isn't so bad," one of the goblins remarked.

"You're right," agreed his friend. "When Jack Frost set up this camp I thought he had a brain freeze. But he was right when he said that holiday camp was fun."

"It's too bad he doesn't want to come out in the sun with us," added another goblin.

The big goblin chuckled. "That's why we had to take Nicki the Holiday Camp Fairy's magic items. If Jack Frost can't have fun in the sun, then nobody will!"

"So that's why he stole the magic items," Kirsty whispered to Rachel.

Rachel looked around. The goblins were still busy with their picture frames.

"Come on," she urged in a whisper. "Let's get that bracelet and get out of here."

The girls tiptoed to the shelf that held the bracelets. Rachel saw the glowing bracelet, reached inside the bin, and slipped it into her pocket. It shone with fairy magic.

The girls hurried towards the front door. But then one of the goblins took a step backwards and bumped into Kirsty. Her fake nose slipped off!

The goblin gasped in surprise.
"Hey, these aren't goblins!" he yelled.
"They're the girls who help the fairies!"
Rachel grabbed Kirsty by the arm.
"Run!" she cried.

A Sticky Escape

"Don't let them escape!" the big goblin shouted.

The goblins raced to the door, blocking the way.

"Quick," Kirsty said, pointing to the back wall and shedding the rest of her goblin costume. "We can climb through that open window."

The girls darted for the window, and Rachel reached it first. She pulled herself up onto the windowsill.

But the goblins were right behind them. Would the girls make it?

"It's time to stop you goblins in your tracks!" a voice cried. It was Nicki! She flew through the window and waved her wand. All of the glue bottles magically floated into the air. They turned upside down, spilling all of the sticky glue onto the floor!

The goblins tried to lift their feet, but they were stuck in the gloopy glue.

"We can't move!" the goblins yelled.

"Rachel, Kirsty, hurry!" Nicki urged.

The girls quickly climbed out of the window and followed Nicki out of the camp and into the woods.

Rachel looked behind her. Some goblins from another cabin were chasing them now!

Kirsty saw them, too. "Maybe we can lose them in the woods!"

They soon reached the trees and hurried down the path. They ran and ran, with Nicki flying behind them.

"Camp Oakwood should be just past those pine trees," Kirsty called out.

But when they passed the pine trees,

there were just more trees. Kirsty stopped
to catch her breath. "That's weird,"
she said. "We should be at the camp
site by now."

"You're right," Nicki agreed. "It feels
like we're going around in circles."

Kirsty slapped her forehead with her
hand. "That's it!" she cried. "Jack Frost
still has the magic compass, which keeps
campers from getting lost."

Nicki started to fly up towards the
trees. "I'll fly overhead and see where
we are."

At that moment, a voice rang through
the air. "Don't move!"

The girls froze. A dozen goblins
emerged from the trees, surrounding
them in a circle.

One of the goblins stepped forwards.

"Give us the magic holiday camp bracelet," he ordered.

"And what if we don't?" Nicki asked.

"Why, we'll— ow!" the goblin yelled.

The rest of the goblins started crying out, too. "Ow! Ow! Ow! Ow!"

Nicki started to laugh. "Look!"

A small army of squirrels had gathered around the goblins. They were pelting the goblins with acorns!

"Run away! Run away!" one of the
goblins yelled.

The goblins scattered, and the squirrels
scampered over to Nicki and the girls.

"Thank you so much, my friends,"
Nicki said. "You know these woods very
well. Can you help us get back to Camp
Oakwood?"

The squirrels made happy chittering sounds and ran ahead. The girls and Nicki followed the cute little creatures through the trees, to the edge of the woods by their camp.

"Thank you!" Rachel and Kirsty called as the squirrels ran off.

Then Rachel reached into her pocket. "This belongs to you, Nicki." She held out the magic holiday camp bracelet.

"Oh, thank you!" Nicki cried happily. "All of the wonderful things I've heard about you girls are true."

She waved her wand
over the bracelet,
and it shrank
down to fairy-size.
Then Nicki placed
it in her backpack.

"From now on, all the activities and
games at camp will be fun," she
promised.

"Rachel! Kirsty!"

The girls spun around. Ellie was
running towards them.

Kirsty looked behind her. "Nicki, you
need to—"

But the little fairy was already gone.

Ellie's brown eyes were shining. "Did
you see that thing with the glittery
wings? I bet it was a fairy!"

"Are you sure it wasn't a butterfly?"
Kirsty asked quickly. "There are a lot of
pretty butterflies around here."

Ellie frowned.

"We can pretend it was a fairy,
though," Rachel told the little girl.
"Why don't we play a game? We'll go
on a fairy search."

"I hope we find one for real!" Ellie
said. She sighed. "I really want fairies
to be real!" She ran ahead, towards the
camp.

"I wish we could tell her that fairies
are real," Rachel whispered.

"Jack Frost is real, too," Kirsty
whispered back. "We need to find
the last two magic items soon, so
everyone can start having fun at Camp
Oakwood!"

Melting Magic

Contents

We're the Fun Foxes!

"Rise and shine, campers!"

The camp leader's cheerful voice rang through the cabin. Rachel sat up slowly, rubbing her eyes. Kirsty put a pillow over her head.

"Is it morning already?" she asked.

"It's morning, and it looks like it's going to be a hot one," Bollie told them.

"But don't worry! We've got lots of fun things planned. Breakfast in fifteen minutes! I don't want my Fun Foxes to be late."

Rachel hopped down from the top bunk. "Wow, Bollie's right," she remarked. "It feels very hot already."

"Well, it's summer. It's supposed to be hot," Kirsty said with a yawn.

The girls changed and headed to the food hall with the rest of the girls from their cabin. Even though it was only the third day of camp, all of the Fun Foxes had become friends. There was red-haired Charlotte; freckly Sophie; Rosie, who made everyone laugh; and Alyssa and Abigail, the twins.

Inside the food hall, the other campers were fanning themselves with their paper plates as they waited in the breakfast queue.

"It's so stuffy in here," Rachel complained.

Kirsty pointed to the corner. "Look. I think the fan is broken."

Two of the camp leaders were standing next to a big fan in the corner.

"It's plugged in, but it won't turn on," one of them was saying.

The girls looked at each other.

"It's the missing water bottle," Rachel whispered. "Nicki says

it helps keep campers cool in the heat."

"We're never going to cool off if we don't get the water bottle back from Jack Frost," Kirsty whispered back.

As the campers ate their eggs, bacon and toast, Bollie made an announcement.

"Attention, campers! The canoes have been fixed. After breakfast, we're all going to the lake so we can beat the heat in the cool water!"

Everyone cheered.

As soon as they finished eating, Kirsty, Rachel, and the other Fun Foxes went back to the cabin to change into swimming costumes and flip-flops. They came back outside carrying towels and bottles of sun cream. Bollie was waiting for them.

"Excellent, Fun Foxes! You're the first ones changed. Line up and follow me," she instructed.

Grinning, they all walked down the sunny path to the lake.

"I'm going to teach you your first camp cheer," Bollie called out. "After I sing a line, I want you to sing it back. Okay?"

"Okay!" the Fun Foxes replied.

Bollie began the cheer, and the campers repeated after her.

"*Everywhere we go!*"
"*Everywhere we go!*"
"*People want to know!*"
"*People want to know!*"
"*Who we are!*"
"*Who we are!*"
"*So we tell them.*"
"*So we tell them.*"
"*We're the Fun Foxes!*"
"*We're the Fun Foxes!*"

"And if they cannot hear us!"
"And if they cannot hear us!"
"We sing a little louder!"
"We sing a little louder!"

The girls repeated the chant again and again, singing louder and louder each time. By the time they reached the lake, they were all giggling. They had almost forgotten how hot they were!

Suddenly, Bollie stopped marching. "Hold on, everybody," she said, putting out an arm to stop the girls. "Something's not right."

She walked closer to the water and then turned back to the campers.

"The lake is even lower than it was yesterday," she said. "It's definitely too low to go canoeing, and it might not be safe to swim in either."

Rachel, Kirsty, and the other Fun
Foxes ran to the shore. Only a few feet
of water covered
the lake bed.

Rachel gasped.
"This is terrible!"

"And it's all Jack
Frost's fault!" Kirsty
whispered to her friend.

Can't Beat the Heat

By this time, the other campers had reached the lake, too. They all groaned when they saw how low the water was.

Bollie and the other leaders huddled together and talked in low voices for a minute. Then they clapped their hands and broke the huddle.

"Okay, campers!" Bollie announced. "Looks like we won't be canoeing or swimming today. Please report to the camp courtyard for a water-balloon fight!"

All of the campers cheered.

"That sounds like fun!" Rachel said.

"And cool, too," agreed Kirsty. She lowered her voice. "I just wish we had a chance to go back to Jack Frost's camp."

"There's nothing we can do until free time," Rachel said. "But I bet Nicki is trying to get the magic water bottle back right now."

"Fun Foxes, line up!" Bollie called out. "Repeat after me: *Everywhere we go...*"

Rachel and Kirsty got in line as the

campers chanted and marched away
from the lake. Campers from the
other cabins joined in, too. The chants
got louder and louder as each cabin
competed to see who could be the
loudest of all.

The campers were hotter than ever
by the time they reached the courtyard
between the camp cabins. Bollie
marched them over to an outdoor tap
at the back of the food hall. One of the

camp leaders came up and handed her a
bag of balloons.

"Let's do this in an assembly line,"
Bollie said. "Rachel and Kirsty, you fill
the balloons with water. Sophie, Alyssa
and Abigail, you tie the knots. Rosie
and Charlotte, see if you can find a
bucket to hold the finished balloons."

Rachel turned on the tap. She held
her hand under the water that trickled
out. It felt ice-cold at first, and Rachel
splashed some on her face to cool off.
But when she put her hand underneath
again, the water was warm.

Rachel frowned. "I don't think this
water-balloon fight is going to
cool us off."

The girls worked together to fill up all
of the water balloons in the bag. Soon

they had a whole bucketful. Around the camp, girls from the other cabins were filling up their balloons, too.

"Okay, Foxes, everybody grab as many balloons as you can," Bollie told them. "We're going to line up around the courtyard."

All of the campers formed a circle in the courtyard. Bollie blew her whistle.

"Let's play!" she cried.

Rachel hurled a balloon across the courtyard. *Splat!* In landed in front of one of the Happy Hedgehog girls, splashing her with water. She laughed and tossed one back.

Splat! The balloon landed in front of Rachel and Kirsty, soaking them. But instead of being cool and refreshing, the water was warm and uncomfortable.

The excitement of the water-balloon fight quickly died down.

"Change of plan!" Bollie announced. "We're sending some of the leaders into town for some ice cream. You've got free time until they come back. I suggest you rest quietly in your cabins. Play a board game or read a book. It's too hot to do anything else!"

The soggy campers shuffled out of the courtyard. Rachel and Kirsty nodded at each other. Instead of going to the cabins, they went right to the woods.

"I hope this is all right," Kirsty said worriedly. "Bollie said we should go to our cabins."

"She *suggested* it," Rachel pointed out. "That's different. Besides, we have to try to get the magic water bottle back. If we don't, we'll never cool off!"

"You're right," Kirsty said, nodding. "Let's go."

They easily found the path that led through the forest. They followed it for a while until the path branched off in four different directions.

Rachel frowned. "I don't remember this part."

"Me, neither," Kirsty said. "Let's pick a path and see where it leads us."

The girls took the second branch on the right and continued through the woods. But they had to stop when the path split again.

"I *definitely* don't remember this," Rachel said.

Kirsty's dark eyes grew wide. "Oh, no! Remember what happened yesterday? Jack Frost has the magic compass that keeps campers from getting lost."

"And now we're lost again!" Rachel cried.

Nicki to the Rescue!

Poof! Just then, Nicki appeared in front of them. The air around her shimmered with fairy magic.

"Oh, girls, I'm so sorry!" she said. "I've spent all morning trying to get into Jack Frost's cabin. But now that he knows we're on to him, he has extra goblin security everywhere."

"Thanks for coming to our rescue," Kirsty said. "We were starting to think we'd never find our way out of these woods."

"I can fly above the trees and lead the way," Nicki told them. "But I don't think there's any point in us going to Camp Frost right now. We need a different plan."

Kirsty looked thoughtful. "If we can't

get into Camp Frost, we have to get the goblins to come out."

"But how can we be sure they'll bring the water bottle with them?" Rachel asked.

Kirsty shrugged. "It's awfully hot today. It seems like they'd carry water everywhere!"

"It won't be easy to get the goblins to leave camp, though," Rachel said.

Nicki fluttered around the girls. "They're very anxious to get the holiday camp bracelet back again. We could use that to lure them out of their camp." She gave her backpack a worried pat. "But that could be dangerous. I'd hate to lose it once more."

"There's lots of glittery thread in our Craft Cabin," Kirsty remembered. "We could make a fake holiday camp bracelet and fool them."

Rachel nodded. "Yes! We could bring a blanket to the edge of the woods and make some bracelets there. I'm sure the goblins will come sniffing around."

Nicki looked excited. "And I can hide in the trees and surprise them! If one of

them has the magic water bottle, I can
shrink it with my wand. Then I'll swoop
down and grab it before they can stop
me!"

"That's a great plan," Rachel agreed.

"But first we have to get back to
camp, and we're lost," Kirsty reminded
the others.

"Not for long!" Nicki sang out
cheerfully. She
flew up, up,
up, above the
trees. "Look
in the sky
and follow the
fairy shimmer!"

The Trap is Set!

The girls looked up and saw what looked like a twinkling star shining over the trees. The star moved down the path, and the girls followed it. Within minutes they were back at camp, thanks to Nicki!

"Wait here, Nicki," Rachel told the fairy. "We'll get the stuff we need and hurry back."

As Rachel and
Kirsty walked to
the Craft Cabin,
they saw some of
the camp leaders pull
into the courtyard in a people carrier.
One got out of the passenger side,
opened the back, and lifted out a big
cool box.

"Ice cream! Get your ice cream!" she
called out.

Kirsty looked at Rachel. "Do you
think the ice cream is okay, or will the
missing magic water bottle ruin it?"

"There's only one way to find out,"
Rachel said, grinning.

They ran to the leader and lined up to
get their ice cream. The leader handed
them each a wooden spoon and a small

cup with the words CHOCOLATE ICE
CREAM on the lid.

"Here goes," Kirsty said. She lifted off
the lid.

"Uh-oh." Rachel looked into her
cup and saw that the ice cream was
bubbling!

"It's hot chocolate!" another one of the
campers wailed.

"It's tasty, but it won't cool us off,"
Kirsty said after taking a sip. She looked
at Rachel. "We'd better hurry up with
our plan."

They ran to the Craft Cabin and collected all the supplies they needed to make bracelets: glittery thread, sparkly beads, scissors, two pieces of cardboard and tape. Then they went to the Fun Foxes' cabin and pulled a small picnic blanket from Kirsty's suitcase.

Once they reached the edge of the woods again, Kirsty spread out the blanket. Both girls sat down and spread out the bracelet-making supplies.

Nicki flew down from the trees, flapping her wings excitedly as she hovered between them.

"There are lots of goblins patrolling the woods, searching for the holiday camp bracelet," she said. "Maybe you could talk in loud voices about the bracelets. If they hear you, I bet they'll come running over."

"Okay," Rachel said. She shivered a little, imagining the goblins running after them.

Nicki saw her shiver. "Don't worry, Rachel. I'll be watching the whole time!"

"First, we need a bracelet that looks like the magic bracelet," Kirsty reminded her.

"Right!" Nicki said. "Leave it to me."

She waved her
wand, and
four pieces
of glittery
thread
floated
up above the
blanket and began to twist around one
another. Small, sparkly beads slid up the
thread as the bracelet took shape.

Seconds later, the shimmering bracelet
floated back down onto the picnic
blanket.

"It's perfect!" Rachel and Kirsty cried
at the same time.

"It's a good copy, but it doesn't have
any magic of its own," Nicki said,
winking. "The goblins will be here soon.
I'd better hide!"

The fairy quickly flew up to her hiding place in the trees.

Rachel chose one pink, one blue, one yellow and one green thread. She cut the threads so they were as long as the space from the tips of her fingers to her elbow. Then she tied the four threads together, at the top. She taped the top to a piece of cardboard to hold it in place and began to weave the threads together, slipping in glittery beads here and there.

"It's great that we can make crafts again," Kirsty said in a loud voice. "Thank goodness Nicki gave us her magic friendship bracelet!"

Kirsty expected the goblins to come charging out at them, but things stayed quiet and peaceful. It was a little bit cooler under the trees, too.

"Making bracelets is fun!" Kirsty said, a little louder this time.

Then they heard something. It was the sound of footsteps in the woods, and the murmur of goblin voices in the air.

"The sound came from over there!" one goblin said.

"Ugh, it's hot today," mumbled another.

A different goblin chimed in. "It's a good thing we've got the magic water bottle with us."

Kirsty glanced up at the trees. Did Nicki hear that, too?

The goblins emerged from the path. The girls could see a shiny water bottle that glittered with fairy magic hanging from a cord around a big goblin's neck.

"He's bringing it right to us," Kirsty whispered to Rachel.

Just then, the big goblin spotted the girls.

"Get the bracelet!" he ordered the others.

A Race Through the Woods

As the goblins raced towards Rachel and Kirsty, Nicki swooped down from the trees. She held her wand out in front of her, and it began to sparkle.

The big goblin was the first to spot her. "Grab her backpack! It's where she keeps the magic items!"

Kirsty picked up the fake friendship bracelet. "No, we have the magic bracelet here!" she cried.

But the goblins were determined to catch Nicki. One of them jumped up and pulled the tiny bag off her back.

"Woo-hoo! I've got it!" he cheered, dangling the tiny backpack from his finger.

Rachel knew she had to do something – and fast!

She charged at the goblin. He stumbled backwards, and the backpack tumbled out of his grasp. Nicki quickly grabbed it and flew out of reach as fast as she could.

"Nicki, keep the backpack safe!" Kirsty called. "We'll get the water bottle."

The big goblin looked down at the

magic water bottle hanging around his neck. "Oh, no you won't!" he promised. Then he turned and ran, with the other goblins right behind him.

"Come on!" Rachel called. "We have to catch them before they get back to Camp Frost!"

The girls ran as fast as they could, but the goblins were faster. Leaves crunched under their feet as they dodged around the trees, trying to catch up to the goblin with the magic water bottle. Soon

the trees began to thin out, and the girls
realised they could see the cabins of
Camp Frost up ahead.

"We're not going to
make it!" Kirsty
cried.

Just then, a
loud cracking
sound filled the
woods. A huge,
old tree branch
crashed down
across the path
ahead! All of the
goblins stumbled over
the fallen branch and
piled up on top of each other.

"Ow! You're stebbing on by
nose!" one goblin complained in a

muffled voice.

"Get your elbow out of my ear!" yelled another.

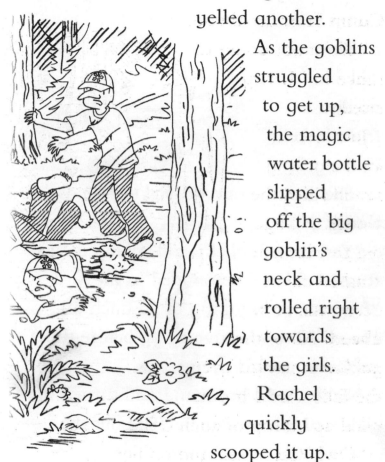

As the goblins struggled to get up, the magic water bottle slipped off the big goblin's neck and rolled right towards the girls. Rachel quickly scooped it up.

"Rachel, look!" Kirsty said, pointing.

A beautiful red, white and black
woodpecker perched
on the fallen
tree branch.
The bird
nodded a
friendly hello
to the girls.

"She must be one of Nicki's friends,"
Kirsty remarked.

"Yes, she is," Nicki said, flying down
to meet them. She nodded to the bird.
"Thanks for breaking the branch off,
Hazel. Now we have to fly before those
goblins untangle themselves!"

Nicki waved her wand and turned the
girls into fairies. Rachel held out the
water bottle. It shrank to fairy-size and
Nicki put it in her backpack.

"After them!" the big goblin yelled, climbing to his feet.

Luckily, the girls could fly much faster than the goblins could run! They soared over the tops of the trees, leaving the angry goblins behind.

As they came to the edge of the woods, Kirsty spotted Ellie by their picnic blanket.

"Rachel! Kirsty! Where are you?" Ellie was calling.

"We'd better change back," Rachel said, fluttering her wings.

"Of course," Nicki said. "And thank you for helping me get the magic water bottle. I think you'll find that things at Camp Oakwood are much cooler now."

The girls and Nicki
flew towards the
ground, making
sure they were
out of Ellie's sight.
Then Nicki waved
her wand, and the
girls changed back to
human-size.

"But we still have to find the missing
magic compass," Rachel reminded them.

Nicki frowned. "I know. But I don't
think we should set another trap for the
goblins. It's too dangerous."

"So what should we do?" Kirsty asked.

"I'm sure we'll think of something,"
Nicki said brightly. "Campers are great
problem-solvers! In the meantime, go
and have some fun. Just be sure to

stay out of the woods until we find the
compass. I don't want you to get lost!"

Nicki waved her wand and
disappeared in a shower of sparkling
fairy dust. Rachel and
Kirsty emerged
from the trees to
find Ellie by the
picnic blanket.

"There you
are!" the little
girl said. "Were
you hunting for fairies? Because I saw
some! I know I did! And they weren't
butterflies. I know because they were
sparkly and shiny. They had to be
fairies."

Had Ellie seen them flying with Nicki?
Suddenly, they heard a loud cheer

coming from the camp. The girls were happy for a distraction, since they couldn't tell Ellie their fairy secret! They rolled up the picnic blanket and ran towards the sound with Ellie alongside them.

All of the campers were racing down the path to the lake. When they reached the shore, Rachel and Kirsty saw what everyone was so happy about. The water level in the lake had risen! It looked nice and deep.

"Good news!" Bollie said. "The water's back. Come and get your feet wet!"

Kirsty and Rachel splashed into the lake. The water felt cool on their skin.

"Things are almost back to normal," Kirsty said.

Rachel nodded. "I can't wait until we get the magic compass back. We'll show Jack Frost that he can't ruin camp!"

Confused
Campers!

Contents

Songs Around the Campfire

"This ice lolly is so cold, I'm getting brain freeze!" Rachel cried, screwing up her face.

Kirsty laughed. "This morning, I thought I would never feel cold again! So I don't mind a little brain freeze."

The girls were slurping on ice lollies in the food hall. The other Fun Foxes were enjoying them, too. Rosie was eating a blackcurrant one. She stuck out her tongue.

"Look! I'm turning purple!" she said, and everyone giggled.

"I'm glad it cooled off before the campfire tonight," said Sophie.

Charlotte nodded. "We all would have melted!"

"I hope we get to sing some of the songs we sang last year," Sophie said.

"Kirsty and I don't know any campfire songs," Rachel told them. "It's our first time at camp."

"They're easy to learn!" Sophie said.

Just then, Ellie ran up to the Fun Foxes table. "Rachel! Kirsty! Do you want to go and look for fairies now?" she asked.

"We'd love to play fairies with you, but it's getting dark," Kirsty told her.

Ellie looked sad.

"We can play tomorrow, okay?" Rachel promised.

Ellie nodded. "Okay," she said softly, walking away.

Kirsty leaned close to Rachel. "That reminds me," she whispered. "We should

try to talk to Nicki before the campfire starts."

The two girls got up. "See you later!" they called to the other Foxes. Then they left the food hall and walked to a quiet spot in a circle of pine trees. The setting sun cast shadows all around them.

"Nicki, are you there?" Rachel asked.

Poof! The tiny fairy appeared in front of them, holding a stick with a marshmallow on top of it. "Hello!" she said with a smile. "I was just about to toast some marshmallows. Is everything all right?"

"We're fine," Kirsty replied.

"And nice and cool, too," Rachel added.

Nicki smiled. "King

Oberon and Queen Titania were so
happy to hear that we got the magic
water bottle back."

"But Jack Frost still has the compass,"
Kirsty reminded her.

"I know," Nicki said with a nod. "But
going after goblins in the dark is never
a good idea. Tonight, you two should
have some fun at camp."

"We're having a sing-along around
the campfire," Rachel told her.

Nicki's eyes lit up. "Oh, I love sing-
alongs!" she said. "Do you think I can
come?"

"You'd have to hide," Kirsty pointed
out.

Nicki looked thoughtful for a moment.
Then she snapped her fingers. Her whole
body began to glow. At the same time,

she got smaller and smaller. Soon she was no bigger than a firefly!

She flew to Kirsty and landed on the tip of her nose. "What do you think?"

"You look just like a firefly," Rachel said. "Lexi the Firefly Fairy would be very impressed!"

"It's a great disguise, but you're making my nose tickle," Kirsty said, giggling. "I think I'm going to sneeze!"

"Sorry!" Nicki said. She flew off

Kirsty's nose and zoomed between the girls, making swirls of light in the air.

The girls walked back to the centre of camp, where the other campers were starting to gather around a bright, orange fire. The sky above was a deep blue, and the first stars were starting to twinkle. Rachel and Kirsty sat on a log together. Kirsty felt Nicki land on her shoulder.

"Okay, campers," Bollie announced. "It's time to sing!"

She started to sing in a loud voice, and the other campers joined in:

"The more we get together,
Together, together.
The more we get together,
The happier we'll be.

For your friends are my friends,
And my friends are your friends.
The more we get together,
The happier we'll be!"

After a while,
Rachel and
Kirsty joined
in, too.

"Sophie
was right,"
Kirsty said.
"It's easy!"

They sang song
after song. Kirsty could hear
Nicki's tiny voice singing along in her
ear. By the time they sang the last song,
the sky was black and a bright moon
shone overhead.

Bollie stood up. "It's time to hit the sack, campers!" she announced. "Cabins, please line up!"

Rachel and Kirsty lined up with the other Fun Foxes. Bollie walked up and started to count them.

"Alyssa, check. Abigail, check. Charlotte, check..."

Suddenly, one of the other leaders let out a yell.

"Oh, no! One of the Happy Hedgehogs is missing!"

A murmur of alarm went through the campers. Bollie frowned and walked over to the camp leader.

"Who's missing?" she asked.

"It's Ellie!" the leader cried.

The Search for Ellie

Rachel and Kirsty gasped.

"She was at the campfire, I'm sure," the leader said. "She must have wandered off."

A girl in the Happy Hedgehogs group tugged on Bollie's shirt.

"I know where she went," the girl said.

"She said she was going into the woods to look for fairies."

"Oh, no!" Rachel turned to her friend. "Kirsty, if she's in the woods, she's going to get lost."

"Nicki, what should we do?" Kirsty whispered.

But then she realised that she couldn't feel Nicki on her shoulder any more. She looked around, but the fairy was gone.

"Maybe she's looking for Ellie," Rachel guessed.

"I hope so," Kirsty said. "We should look for her, too."

But Bollie blew her whistle. "I want all campers in their cabins right now! Leaders, when everyone is safely inside we're going to form a search party."

The girls had no choice. They marched

quickly back to their cabin.

The other Fun Foxes were worried, too.

"I hope Ellie will be all right," said Abigail.

"I'm sure the leaders will find her," Charlotte chimed in.

Rachel and Kirsty looked at each other.

"Jack Frost has the magic compass," Kirsty said in a low voice. "That means the leaders are going to get lost, too!"

"I know," Rachel said. "We have to help!"

Rachel and Kirsty didn't want to disobey their camp leader. But this was an emergency! While the other girls

in the cabin talked and changed into pyjamas, they tiptoed out of the cabin.

The girls hurried towards the woods. They could see the yellow glow of torches as Bollie and two other leaders searched the trails.

"Ellie! Where are you?" the leaders called out.

A bright firefly flew towards Rachel and Kirsty in the dark, growing bigger and bigger as it got closer. But it wasn't a firefly at all — it was Nicki!

"Sorry I left so quickly, but I was hoping to find Ellie before she got too far," Nicki explained, looking serious. "I haven't found her yet, but I did find someone who can help."

As she spoke, a huge owl swooped down from the sky and landed on a nearby tree branch. The owl had golden feathers. His yellow eyes glowed brightly in his face.

"This is Midnight," Nicki said. "He can see at night, so he'll help us find Ellie. But you two will need to fly."

She took some fairy dust from her backpack and poured it into her palm.

Then she blew on it, sprinkling glittery
sparkles all over the girls. They quickly
turned into fairies!

The girls and Nicki flew over to
Midnight and sat on his back. The owl's
feathers felt soft
but strong
under their
fingers. They
held on tightly

as the owl took off,
soaring high above the trees. Midnight
flew much faster than the girls could fly
on their own!

"This is a bit scary!" Kirsty cried,
as the air pushed her hair straight out
behind her.

Rachel grinned and cheered. "I wish
we could go this fast all the time!"

Just then, Midnight began to fly in a
circle. He had spotted Ellie!

"There she is!" Nicki cried, pointing
down. The scared little girl was sitting
at the base of a tree, crying. "Midnight,
please let us down nearby. We can't let
Ellie see us yet."

The owl slowly flew down to the forest
floor. Rachel and Kirsty hopped off his
back.

"Thank you, Midnight," Kirsty said.

"I'll change you back," Nicki told
the girls, waving her wand. "Go and
get Ellie, and then look for Midnight in
the trees. He'll lead you safely back to
camp."

The girls nodded and ran off towards
the sound of Ellie's sobbing. Her face
brightened when she saw them.

"Rachel! Kirsty! You found me!" she cried, jumping to her feet. She threw her arms around Rachel. "I was looking for fairies, but I didn't find any. Then I got lost!"

"You're not lost any more," Rachel said. "Come on, let's get back to camp."

Kirsty heard a rustle and saw that Midnight had landed in a tree nearby.

"It's this way," Kirsty said.

The girls followed Midnight down the

path. The owl flew quietly and slowly ahead of them, showing them the way.

After a few minutes, they heard voices up ahead and saw the glow of torches. Bollie and the other two leaders were arguing about which way to go. Then Bollie spotted the girls coming down the path. "Oh my gosh! Ellie!"

Ellie ran up to Bollie and hugged her.

"I'm so glad you're safe!" Bollie said. Then she nodded to Rachel and Kirsty. "What are you two doing out here?"

"We heard Ellie crying from our cabin," Kirsty said, thinking quickly.

"So we ran towards the sound," Rachel added.

Bollie frowned. "I know you were just trying to help. But you should never come into the woods at night. What if you had got lost, too?"

"Speaking of which," said one of the leaders, "how do we get back to camp?"

Kirsty spotted Midnight down the path on the right. "I'm pretty sure it's this way. Follow me."

Thanks to Midnight, the girls and leaders got safely back to camp. Rachel and Kirsty went straight to their cabin, but before they went inside, they looked up at the sky. Midnight was circling overhead, a tiny bright light following behind him.

"Thanks, Midnight," Rachel whispered.

"You, too, Nicki," Kirsty added.

Get that Compass!

Rachel and Kirsty talked quietly together at breakfast the next morning.

"Ellie could have been hurt in the woods last night," Rachel said with concern.

Kirsty nodded. "Jack Frost has gone too far. It's one thing to spoil everyone's fun, but now he's putting some campers in danger!"

After breakfast, Bollie made an
announcement.

"In one hour we'll be starting our
volleyball tournament," she said. "You
have free time until then."

"Perfect!" Kirsty said to Rachel.

They put away their breakfast dishes
and raced to the edge of the woods.

"Nicki? Are you there?" Rachel called
out.

They heard a noise from one of the
trees and looked up to see Nicki chatting
with a robin on a branch. She flew
down when she saw the girls.

"I had a feeling I'd see you two this
morning," she said, smiling.

"We need to find the magic compass,
fast!" said Rachel.

"I know," Nicki said. "But the goblins

are guarding Jack Frost's camp. It won't be easy."

"Still, we have to try," Kirsty said.

"Now that's what I call camp spirit!" Nicki cried. "Follow me, girls! Midnight helped me make a trail last night."

She pointed her magic wand at the path. Glittery craft beads lined the trail.

"See? We just follow the beads!" Nicki said happily.

The path took them straight to the Ice Lord's Camp Frost.

But before they could hide, they heard a voice above them. "Those girls are back! Everyone to your positions!"

"Oh, no!" Nicki cried. "Jack Frost has goblin guards in the trees!"

A small army of goblins ran out of the cabins. Each one held a slingshot, and they started shooting acorns at Nicki and the girls!

"Run!" Rachel yelled.

The girls ran as fast as they could, with Nicki flying right behind them. They didn't stop until they reached the edge of their own camp.

"That was close," Rachel said, catching her breath.

"You're telling me," Kirsty said. "We need a way to get past those guards."

"But for now, you girls had better go back to camp," Nicki told them. "I'll meet you back here when you have more free time."

Rachel and Kirsty nodded and waved as they ran off.

Back at camp, they found Bollie playing with Ellie and some of the young campers in the playground.

Ellie was telling the others about her adventure the night before.

"I didn't see any fairies, but I saw another camp on the other side of the woods," Ellie was saying. "There were a bunch of boys wearing green uniforms."

Rachel nudged Kirsty. Ellie must have seen the goblins!

"That sounds like a Forest Scout

camp," Bollie said. "There used to be
a boys' camp on the other side of the
woods, but it closed years ago. They
must have reopened it." The camp leader
smiled at the group. "I remember when I
was your age. The girls raided the boys'
camp with water balloons. That was a
lot of fun."

"That does sound like fun," Rachel
agreed, grinning.

Bollie snapped her fingers. "I've got it!
We should raid the Forest Scouts' camp
today!"

"Oh, no," Kirsty said under her breath.
She looked at Rachel with wide eyes.

If Bollie carried out her idea, she
would be leading the campers straight to
Jack Frost and his goblins!

Girls vs Goblins

"Are you sure that raiding the boys' camp is a good idea?" Kirsty asked nervously.

"Of course!" Bollie said. "It's a camp tradition!"

Rachel pulled Kirsty aside. "Maybe it's not so bad," she whispered. "There are lots of goblins, and only you, me and

Nicki to face them. If all of the girls here raid the camp, we might be able to get past the goblin guards. Then we could get to the magic compass."

"But then everyone will know that goblins are real," Kirsty reminded her.

Rachel frowned. "I forgot about that."

Kirsty was thoughtful. "You know, the goblins look a lot like ordinary boys when you first see them. Maybe we could do the raid when it's starting to get dark, so none of the girls can see them very well."

Rachel nodded. "Good idea!"

The girls walked back over to Bollie.

"A raid would be fun," Kirsty said. "What if we do it around sunset tonight?

That will give us time to plan."

"That sounds great," Bollie agreed. "We can work out our plan this afternoon."

"And we know how to get to the boys' camp," Rachel quickly added, thinking of the trail of beads. "We saw it last night when we found Ellie."

"Perfect!" Bollie said.

The next few hours went by like a normal camp day. They played volleyball, ate lunch, and started weaving potholders in the Craft Cabin. Then Bollie called all of the older campers together for a meeting in the food hall.

"Here's the plan," she said. "The Forest Scouts have a camp on the other side of the woods. Right after dinner, we're going to raid them. We'll run up to the camp, pelt them with water balloons, and then make a run for it." She held up a plastic carrier bag filled with packages of balloons. "We've got a lot of balloons to fill!"

The Fun Foxes set up next to the outdoor tap and started an assembly line, filling up balloon after balloon. When they had no empty balloons left, Rachel and Kirsty walked around the side of the food hall.

Before they could call Nicki's name, the fairy appeared in front of them. Her wings now looked like the wings of an orange-and-black butterfly!

"I know about the

plan," she said. "I've been disguised as a butterfly all day, listening in."

She waved her wand, and her wings turned back to their normal colour.

"Bollie is a great leader," Nicki went on. "This plan is just what we needed! While the goblins are dodging water balloons, the three of us can go and look for the magic compass."

The fairy winked and disappeared, and the girls headed into the food hall for dinner. Everyone was so excited about the raid that they could barely eat their chicken and mashed potatoes!

When dinner was cleared away, Bollie blew her whistle. "Older girls from the Fun Foxes, Merry Mice and Happy Hedgehogs, line up for the big raid!"

The older girls clapped and cheered

Bollie motioned to Rachel and Kirsty. "You two, front of the line," she said. "We need you to lead the way."

The other campers grabbed buckets of water balloons and lined up behind Rachel and Kirsty. They walked to the woods and then headed down the path lined with glittering beads.

"Can we sing a camp song?" Rosie asked.

"Not this time," Bollie told her. "We want this to be a surprise."

"It won't be much of a surprise if those goblin guards are still in the trees," Kirsty murmured to Rachel.

Soon they came to the trail near Camp Frost. Rachel and Kirsty looked up. There was no sign of the goblin guards yet.

"Luckily, goblins are lazy," Rachel told Kirsty in a low voice. "They must be taking a break."

Kirsty turned to Bollie. "We'll go up ahead and scout things out."

The two girls carefully made their way along the path. Through the trees, they could see goblins outside the cabins. They were playing volleyball. Or trying to!

"Ow! You threw the ball at my nose!" one goblin complained.

"It slipped out of my fingers!" another goblin protested.

"They're arguing! Perfect," Kirsty said, just as Nicki appeared in a cloud of sparkles.

"Are we ready to go?" Nicki asked.

The girls nodded.

"I'll go and tell Bollie," Rachel said, running back down the path.

A few seconds later, Bollie and the other campers came jogging towards Camp Frost.

"Camp Oakwood is the best! Better than all the rest!" Bollie chanted. The other girls joined in.

The goblins froze. They stopped arguing and looked towards the forest. Then...SPLAT! The water balloons started flying!

"Ugh! It's clean water!" a goblin yelled.

"Run for cover!" the other goblins cried.

Rachel and Kirsty knew they had to act quickly, while

the goblins were distracted. They ran towards the cabins.

"I'm sure Jack Frost has the magic compass in his cabin," Nicki said, appearing in the air next to them.

As they reached the main cabin, Rachel threw open the door. A blast of freezing cold air rushed out. Just inside the door, a tall man with spiky white hair faced them.

"Jack Frost!" Kirsty cried.

The wicked Ice Lord held up his hand and opened his palm. The magic compass glittered against his pale skin.

"Are you looking for this?" he asked with a grin.

A Tricky Deal

Nicki bravely flew right up to Jack Frost.

"Give that back!" she said firmly. "The magic compass doesn't belong to you."

Jack Frost just laughed. "It's mine now, little fairy!"

"But that compass keeps campers from getting lost," Rachel told him. "And last night, Ellie got lost in the woods."

"She could have been hurt,"
Kirsty added. "That's just
plain mean, Jack Frost!"

"*Hmph!*" Jack Frost scowled.
"I just wanted to have fun
camping, like everybody else!"

"Why can't you have fun
camping?" Kirsty asked.

"Oh, I can make crafts and swim
in a lake if I want to," Jack Frost
replied, rolling his eyes. "But at night,
campers sit around a campfire and roast
marshmallows and sing songs. I can't do
that, because the fire is too hot!"

"So you wanted to ruin everyone else's
time at camp, just because you can't sit
around a campfire?" Rachel asked.

Jack Frost nodded. Suddenly, he
reached out and grabbed Nicki from the

air. "And now, I'll take back that magic bracelet and water bottle!"

Nicki struggled to get free from Jack Frost's grip. He reached for her backpack with a long, pointy finger.

"Wait!" Kirsty cried. "Why don't we do a deal?"

The Ice Lord stopped. "What kind of deal?" he asked frostily.

Kirsty raised an eyebrow. "I bet Nicki could make you a magic fire that feels cold, not hot. Couldn't you, Nicki?"

The little fairy nodded. "Of course! Campfire magic is one of my favourites!"

"With a magic fire, you and your goblins could toast marshmallows and sing campfire songs all night long," Kirsty told Jack Frost.

163

His pale eyes gleamed with excitement. "That would be wonderful!"

"I'll only do it if you give me the magic compass," Nicki said. "Do we have a deal?"

Jack Frost was silent for a moment. Then he opened his palm and freed Nicki. "Deal!" he said.

Nicki flew up into the air and waved her magic wand. Glittery blue sparks whirled around her as she began her fairy spell.

"Fire, fire, burn so nice.
Burn with flames as cold as ice!"

Poof! A roaring campfire appeared outside the door of Jack Frost's cabin. He slowly walked up to it and passed his

hand over the flames.

"They're positively freezing!" he cried. "How marvellous!"

"Now it's time to keep your end of the bargain," Rachel reminded him.

Jack Frost held out the magic compass. Nicki waved her wand over it, shrank it down to fairy-size, and slipped it in her backpack.

"Come on," Kirsty said. "Let's go before he changes his mind."

The girls ran outside to see the goblins

still fleeing from the water balloons. They were all bumping into one another!

Then Bollie blew her whistle. "We're out of balloons, girls! Let's retreat!"

The girls turned and raced back down the forest path, hollering and squealing with excitement.

"I'll catch up with you later," Nicki told Rachel and Kirsty, grinning from ear to ear. "I'm going to tell the king and queen that we found the magic compass!"

The fairy vanished in a whirl of sparkles, and the girls chased after the other campers.

By the time they got back to camp, it was dark. Some of the other leaders had started a campfire.

"Great raid, girls!" Bollie said, catching her breath. "Let's celebrate with some toasted marshmallows!"

"This is delicious!" Kirsty said after her first bite.

"I wonder if Jack Frost likes toasted marshmallows?" Rachel asked with a smile.

The happy chatter of the campers filled the camp. Then, in the distance, the girls heard a strange howling.

"What's that?" Bollie wondered.

The girls fell quiet as they listened. It sounded like boys singing in horrible, off-key voices.

"The more we get together,
Together, together.
The more we get together,
The nastier we'll be!"

Bollie shook her head. "Sounds like those Forest Scouts to me."

Rachel and Kirsty looked at each other and grinned. They knew the truth. Those terrible singers were goblins!

The next morning, the girls woke to bright sunshine streaming through their cabin windows. The other Fun Foxes were still asleep. Suddenly, a robin appeared at the window. She gently tapped her beak against the glass.

"That looks like Nicki's friend," Kirsty said.

The two girls quietly went outside and sat on the cabin steps. Nicki flew up.

"Rise and shine, campers!" she said cheerfully. "I have something for you."

Nicki opened her backpack and took out three glittery bracelets.

"Ooh, they look just like the magic bracelet!" Kirsty cried happily.

"There's one for each of you, and one for Ellie," Nicki said. "King Oberon and Queen Titania felt terrible when they heard how she got lost."

"Thank you so much, Nicki!" Rachel said.

Nicki gave each girl a kiss on the

cheek. "Thanks to you, campers everywhere will have a great time this summer!"

"Will we see you again?" Kirsty asked.

Nicki nodded. "If you need me, just call my name. But right now, I've got to go and referee a game of volleyball."

The fairy flew up towards the trees. The robin joined her, and the two of them swooped and swirled in the sky.

"See you soon, Nicki!" Rachel and Kirsty called, waving.

The girls spotted Ellie a little while later at breakfast. Rachel winked at Kirsty, then handed Ellie one of the special holiday camp bracelets.

"This is for you," she said. "It's just like ours, see?"

Ellie's eyes widened. "It's so pretty! It looks just like a magic fairy bracelet. Do you think fairies are real?"

Rachel and Kirsty smiled at each other. They could never tell Ellie their secret. But they didn't need to.

"They're real if you believe in them," Rachel said.

Kirsty nodded. "Rachel's right. If you believe in fairies, they'll always be with you."

Ellie smiled. "I knew it!"

Now it's time for Kirsty and
Rachel to help...

Carly the schoolfriend Fairy

Read on for a sneak peek...

Rachel Walker strolled over to the grand
doors of Tippington Town Hall and
peered outside. There were minibuses
pulling up and lots of people milling
around, but no sign of the very special
person she was looking for!

Rachel's school was taking part in
an exciting competition. Four schools
from different parts of the country were
competing in two different events. A
spelling bee was to be held today at the
Town Hall, and a science contest was
to take place at the Science Museum

tomorrow. And at the end of the week, there would be a disco at Rachel's school!

Rachel was part of the Tippington School spelling bee team, but the most exciting thing was that Kirsty's School, Wetherbury High, was also taking part in the competition. Kirsty was part of the science team and this meant that she was coming to Tippington!

Read **Carly the Schoolfriend Fairy** to find out what adventures are in store for Kirsty and Rachel!

RAINBOW magic ®

Meet the fairies, play games
and get sneak peeks at
the latest books!

www.rainbowmagicbooks.co.uk

There's fairy fun for everyone on
our wonderful website.
You'll find great activities, competitions, stories and
fairy profiles, and also a special newsletter.

Get 30% off all Rainbow Magic books at

www.rainbowmagicbooks.co.uk

Enter the code RAINBOW at the checkout.
Offer ends 31 December 2013.

Offer valid in United Kingdom and Republic of Ireland only.

Competition!

This is a competition from Kirsty and Rachel especially for you!

When you have read all three stories in Nicki the Holiday Camp Fairy, go back and have a careful look at the pictures.

There are six acorns hidden in this special Rainbow Magic book, and each one has a letter in it. Find all six letters and rearrange them to make a special Fairyland word, and then send it to us.

Clue:
These are what you sleep in at camp

We will put the correct entries into a draw and select one winner to receive a special Rainbow Magic goody bag. Your name will also be featured in a forthcoming Rainbow Magic story!

Enter online now at www.rainbowmagicbooks.co.uk

No purchase required. Only one entry per child.
Two prize draws will take place on 30th August 2013 and 30th November 2013. Alternatively readers can send the answer on a postcard to: Rainbow Magic Nicki the Holiday Camp Fairy Competition, Orchard Books, 338 Euston Road, London, NW1 3BH.
Australian readers can write to: Rainbow Magic Nicki the Holiday Camp Fairy Competition, Hachette Children's Books, level 17/207 Kent St, Sydney, NSW 2000.
E-mail: childrens.books@hachette.com.au.
New Zealand readers should write to: Rainbow Magic Nicki the Holiday Camp Fairy Competition, 4 Whetu Place, Mairangi Bay, Auckland, NZ

Carly the
Schoolfriend Fairy

It's time to visit fairy school with
a brand-new Rainbow Magic friend!

www.rainbowmagicbooks.co.uk